A DOLL FOR GRANDMA

A Story about Alzheimer's Disease

by Paulette Bochnig Sharkey   illustrated by Samantha Woo

beaming books
MINNEAPOLIS

For Brian, dearly missed
—PBS

Text copyright © 2020 Paulette Bochnig Sharkey
Illustrations copyright © 2020 Beaming Books

Published in 2020 by Beaming Books, an imprint of 1517 Media.
Printed in the United States of America

26 25 24 23 22 21 20   1 2 3 4 5 6 7 8

ISBN: 978-1-5064-5738-3

Written by Paulette Bochnig Sharkey
Illustrated by Samantha Woo

Library of Congress Cataloging-in-Publication Data

Names: Sharkey, Paulette Bochnig, author. | Woo, Samantha, illustrator.
Title: A doll for grandma / by Paulette Bochnig Sharkey ; illustrated by
   Samantha Woo.
Description: Minneapolis, MN : Beaming Books, 2020. | Audience: Ages 4-8. |
   Summary: Kiera and her grandmother have always been very close, so when
   Grandma's brain forgets how to remember and she must go to a nursing
   home, Kiera finds a new way to connect.
Identifiers: LCCN 2019031890 | ISBN 9781506457383 (hardcover)
Subjects: CYAC: Grandmothers--Fiction. | Memory--Fiction. | Nursing
   homes--Fiction. | Old age--Fiction.
Classification: LCC PZ7.1.S4836 Dol 2020 | DDC [E]--dc23
LC record available at https://lccn.loc.gov/2019031890

VN0004589; 9781506457383; MAR2020

Beaming Books
510 Marquette Avenue
Minneapolis, MN 55402
Beamingbooks.com

Kiera and Grandma always found
ways to have fun together.

They played dress-up. Grandma's feet were so tiny her fancy shoes almost fit Kiera.

They painted their fingernails in shiny, bright colors. Grandma's nails were long and made a *rat-a-tat-tat* sound on the table.

They zipped around in Grandma's sporty car.

When Kiera stayed overnight at Grandma's house, Grandma knit while they watched TV. She showed Kiera how to weave and loop yarn on her fingers to make a necklace.

On special occasions, they baked molasses cookies using an old recipe from Grandma's mother. Kiera pinched off bits of dough and rolled them into perfect balls.

They served the cookies at their picnics.
Kiera's doll was invited.

"What's special about today?" Kiera asked.

"You are, Kiera," Grandma said.

One day, Kiera saw Grandma's keys
in the refrigerator next to the orange juice.

And Grandma started knitting hats
too small to fit anyone's head.

"I think something's wrong with Grandma," Kiera told her mom.

"Grandma's brain is forgetting how to remember," Mom explained.

Soon Grandma moved into
a place for people who had
trouble remembering.

When Kiera visited Grandma
at the memory-care home,
Grandma was different.

Instead of fancy high heels, she wore thick gray shoes with Velcro straps.

Instead of knitting when she watched TV, she rubbed her hands over her blanket, pulling off fuzzy tufts of yarn and piling them in her lap.

Kiera noticed that the nails on Grandma's busy fingers were bare and cut short.

No more *rat-a-tat-tat*.

Instead of driving her sporty car,
Grandma traveled by wheelchair.

Most days Grandma stared out
the window and didn't say much.

Once in a while, she said something that made Kiera laugh.

One afternoon Grandma announced, "I had fried mosquitoes and a cup of hot tea for lunch."

"Was it good?" asked Kiera.

"Delicious." Grandma smiled, but her lips quickly settled back into a straight line. Kiera missed Grandma's smile.

Another day, Grandma called Kiera "Sally Mae."

What's going on? Kiera wondered.

On the way home Mom said, "Sally Mae was Grandma's best friend when she was about your age."

That gave Kiera an idea.

Kiera and Mom went to the store.
They picked out a baby doll for Grandma.

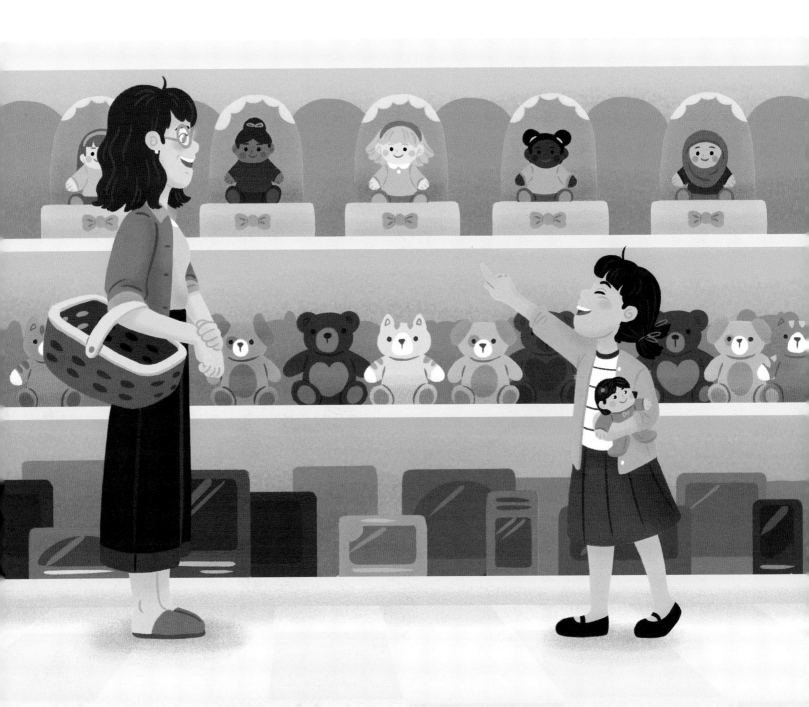

Grandma cried when they gave it to her,
but Kiera thought she looked happy.

Kiera and Grandma took care of their dolls together, rocking them and feeding them and tucking them in for naps.

They all went to listen when the piano lady came. Grandma sat quietly until she heard "You Are My Sunshine." Then she sang LOUD, serenading her doll and everybody else.

On Saturday afternoons, volunteers brought their dogs.

"Oh, puppy, puppy, puppy," Grandma whispered, stroking a tiny dog's silky ears. She showed her doll how to pet the puppy, too.

On special occasions, Kiera and Mom baked
molasses cookies to share with Grandma.
They followed the old recipe exactly.

"Know what's special about today, Grandma?"
Kiera asked.

"You are."

Helping Children Understand Alzheimer's Disease

Currently about 8.3 million Americans are living with dementia; nearly 70 percent of these people are experiencing the type of dementia caused by Alzheimer's disease. By sharing some of these tips with children, you can help them understand what's happening—and help the whole family continue to communicate their love.

Dementia takes away the ability to remember, not just a person's memories.

When our brains are healthy, it's good to exercise our memory. But people with dementia begin to lose this ability to access the past. Trying to jog their memory with clues or questions only shows them that their skills are failing. It's better to share our own memories.

Instead of asking, "Grandma, don't you remember…?" we can say, "Oh, Grandma, I remember when…!" When we love someone experiencing dementia, we can become their memory keepers and storytellers. If Grandma doesn't have beautiful fingernails anymore, tell her the story of how much fun it was to paint nails together. Rather than being sad about what's no longer possible, retell your and their happiest memories and accomplishments.

Dementia takes away our ability to recognize reality.

Dementia takes away the skills a person needs to correctly understand what is happening in the present. Our memory and ability to compare our thoughts with what others say and do helps us properly interpret what's true. When someone loses their memory and rational thinking skills to dementia, they lose reality.

The best response is to follow Kiera's lead: accept your loved one's reality and enjoy it with them. Talk about what you can see and hear around you. Bring whatever your loved one finds pleasing or beautiful. Sensory stimulation becomes more enjoyable than conversation, so dolls, music, animals—anything that will bring them happiness—will enhance your time together.

Dementia takes away language—but not all communication.

Dementia takes away a person's vocabulary as their memory and rational thinking skills fade. However, they do not lose the ability to understand or communicate nonverbal messages, such as tone, expression, and gestures. Those abilities are part of a person's intuitive thinking skills. What you say will become less important than how you say it. Your loved one will increasingly confuse words and meanings yet continue to recognize emotions. And people never stop feeling their own emotions, even when they can no longer express how they feel through words.

Dementia takes away the ability to change one's own moods.

The loss of memory and rational thinking skills also affects a person's ability to manage their moods, while increasing their confusion, frustration, and fear. The greatest gifts we bring to our loved ones with dementia are the uplifting moods that they can no longer create for themselves.

When you're with your loved one, put away your frustration, sorrow, and guilt. If you concentrate on expressing serenity rather than concern, you'll find peace and comfort together. Even with dementia, people can enjoy positive emotions whenever their companions bring such feelings to share.

 **JUDY CORNISH** is the founder of the Dementia & Alzheimer's Well Being Network® (DAWN) and the author of two books: *The Dementia Handbook* and *Dementia with Dignity*. Previously, she worked in vocational rehabilitation with people who had brain injuries and was a licensed attorney and member of the National Academy of Elder Law Attorneys. She left her law practice to work with people in her community who were experiencing dementia and wanted to continue living in their own homes. What she learned from them became the DAWN Method®.

ABOUT THE
AUTHOR AND ILLUSTRATOR

PAULETTE BOCHNIG SHARKEY is the author of dozens of articles and puzzles for children's magazines. *A Doll for Grandma* is her first picture book. Her inspiration for this story came from working as a volunteer pianist with memory-care residents and from caring for family members with dementia. Both brought moments of great joy and fulfillment. Paulette lives in East Lansing, Michigan, with her husband and their big grey cat, and travels to visit her daughter and grandson as often as possible. They often bake molasses cookies together, using an old family recipe.

SAMANTHA WOO lives in Southern California and studied illustration at the Laguna College of Art + Design. Her passion is shared between creating simple, bright, and colorful story book illustrations and designing greeting cards and stationery.